Anonymous

Complimentary Dinner to Stephen N. Gifford

Clerk of the Massachusetts Senate - In Honor of his Twenty-Five Years'

Service in that Capacity.

Anonymous

Complimentary Dinner to Stephen N. Gifford
Clerk of the Massachusetts Senate - In Honor of his Twenty-Five Years' Service in that Capacity.

ISBN/EAN: 9783337159085

Printed in Europe, USA, Canada, Australia, Japan

Cover: Foto ©Andreas Hilbeck / pixelio.de

More available books at **www.hansebooks.com**

COMPLIMENTARY DINNER

TO

STEPHEN N. GIFFORD, Esq.,

CLERK OF THE MASSACHUSETTS SENATE,

IN HONOR OF HIS TWENTY-FIVE YEARS' SERVICE IN THAT CAPACITY,
GIVEN BY THE MEMBERS OF THE SENATE DURING THAT PERIOD,

AT THE UNITED STATES HOTEL, BOSTON,

MARCH 10, 1882.

From a Phonographic Report.

BOSTON:

PRESS OF GEO. H. ELLIS, 141 FRANKLIN STREET.

1883.

In Honor

OF THE FAITHFUL SERVICE OF A TRUE MAN, WHO FOR MANY YEARS
HAS ADORNED THE TRUST REPOSED IN HIM BY EVERY QUALITY
WHICH SHOULD DISTINGUISH THE PUBLIC SERVICE
AND EVERY GRACE OF CHARACTER WHICH
CAN ATTACH HIM TO HIS ASSOCIATES.

CORRESPONDENCE.

STEPHEN N. GIFFORD, Esq. :

Dear Sir,— In recognition of your long and valuable service to the Commonwealth as Clerk of the Massachusetts Senate, and also, and not less, in the exercise of those feelings of earnest friendship and regard which so many years of delightful personal intercourse have engendered, the undersigned, a committee for that purpose, tender to you, on behalf of themselves and their associates,— members of the Senate for the last twenty-five years, —a complimentary dinner, to be given, if agreeable to you, at the United States Hotel, in Boston, March 10, at five o'clock P.M.

Will you please inform us whether the time will suit your convenience, and oblige,

Very respectfully and cordially yours,

ROBERT R. BISHOP,
JOSEPH BENNETT,
GEO. G. CROCKER, } *Committee.*
ANDREW C. STONE,
FRANCIS W. ROCKWELL,

Boston, Feb. 26, 1882.

GENTLEMEN,— Your note of the 17th inst. is received; and, in reply, I assure you that I am deeply grateful for your very kind expressions of regard for myself personally, and for the generous estimation of my services during my long official connection with the Senate. I deem myself most fortunate to have an opportunity to greet once more the friends of past years, and I gladly accept the invitation so kindly extended to meet you and them at the time and place named in your note.

Yours very truly,

S. N. GIFFORD.

Hon. ROBERT R. BISHOP and others.

DINNER.

In response to the invitation of the Committee of Arrangements, over two hundred members of the Senate, from 1858 to 1882 inclusive, and including members from each Senate during that period, sat down to the dinner in honor of the veteran Clerk. Hon. WILLIAM CLAFLIN, the senior living President of the Senate during that period in the country, presided.

After the company had assembled in the dining-hall, the President invited Rev. Edmund Dowse, of Sherborn, Chaplain of the Senate, to invoke the divine blessing, which he did as follows : —

INVOCATION BY REV. EDMUND DOWSE.

Almighty God, we thank thee for this suspension of business, of burdens and cares, for a season of rational and healthful recreation. We thank thee that so large a number who have been associated together in public life have convened on this occasion to renew acquaintance, to strengthen friendships, and more especially to testify their respect and esteem for him who, for a quarter of a century annually, they have chosen to make a record of their legislative acts ; and, while we gratefully acknowledge thee, in view of his long, faithful, and successful service, we desire to commend him to thy Fatherly care in the future, asking that thou wilt grant him length of days, a competence of worldly good, all merited honors, and a final approval of thee.

Grant that thy servants may go away from this occasion refreshed for the duties of life, and that we may ever remain loyal to the interests of the State, of our country, of the great human brotherhood, and to thee, the God and Father of us all; and thine shall be the praise forever. Amen.

After the dinner was concluded, the President again asked the attention of the company, and spoke as follows:—

ADDRESS OF HON. WILLIAM CLAFLIN.

Gentlemen, members of the present and past Senates of the State of Massachusetts, I meet you with sincere pleasure to-night for the purpose of congratulating you and our guest upon his quarter of a century of continuous public service [applause], an occasion which has never occurred in the past, and certainly will very rarely in the future. No predecessor of his has occupied his position for more than half that time. The gentleman who has succeeded in securing for twenty-five years the ballots of the Senate of Massachusetts must be possessed of rare qualities [applause], of good sense, of thorough knowledge, and devotion to the duties of the position which he has held. [Applause.]

Massachusetts has always had the idea of continuous public service, wherever she could find a gentleman that performed the duties of his office to her acceptance. Evidence of this is seen in the town elections all over the State, where we find gentlemen holding office from twenty to thirty, and sometimes forty, years; so that civil service reform does belong to the sentiment of Massachusetts. We are in favor of it. We expect that our Senators in Congress and our Representatives will, to the best of their ability, promote it, until the subordinate positions are taken from the arena of politics, and men are left free to assert their principles and perform their duties in Congress without the pressure of public office driving them in this direction or in that direction. [Applause.]

I only intend to detain you a few moments, for we have too many gentlemen from whom you will desire to hear; but I must say in passing that there is no more agreeable public position for those who occupy it than a position in the Senate of Massachusetts. The body is large enough for active work, it is small enough for every one to keep thoroughly acquainted with his associates. From its numbers have been taken men for all positions in the country. It is a high and honorable position, and every man who has had the honor to occupy it must feel gratified that the time has been when he could be one of the Senate of the State; and he must look back to it, years afterward, with satisfaction. To be sure, the Senate is so pleasant a body that sometimes we think that our Senators, and also our Representatives, like to stay a little longer in the season than they have reason to; and I am sometimes afraid that that reform which I have so many years advocated of biennial sessions has been kept back by this desire of our friends. [Laughter.] But I should not do them the injustice of saying this is so; but I trust that this reform, which seems to me so essential to the politics of almost all of the States of the Union, will be as far perfected as it is possible for the Legislature to do it this year, in order that the people of this State may say by their votes at the proper time whether or not we shall have an annual or biennial session. [Applause.]

In former times, when we met at the State House, and stayed some thirty or sixty days, it did not much matter,— the expense to the State was not a great consideration. It is not that which is our trouble: it is the trouble of sending you there, gentlemen,— the trouble of the long session and constant change of the law. These things should be altered. The time has now come, it seems to me, when this reform, so much to be desired, should be accomplished.

But I will pass on to say one or two other things in regard to our State. Certainly, we must be satisfied with her prosperity and growth in the past. You are called upon at the present session of the Senate to apportion the State for twelve Representatives in Congress,— an encouraging increase, taking into consideration the small area of our State, our confined space, and our freedom from mines and other things of that nature that tend to add to the population of other States. It is a wonderful fact that this State should keep up its numbers in proportion with the other flourishing States of the country,— that, while the country has grown from forty to fifty millions in ten years, we have been able to increase our number in proportion. We are proud of the position which we hold in Congress; and, to aid in the great discussions which have been going on in regard to the rights of certain foreign people, Massachusetts has held up her old ideas by her Senators firmly. And, to the honor of the State, they undoubtedly will sustain them to the end. [Applause.]

Gentlemen, it is with the sincerest regret that I cannot bring to you to-night our respected Chief Magistrate, who is always welcome on all such occasions when the people are assembled. He has kindly sent a letter, which I will take the opportunity to read, showing his good feeling toward our guest : —

HON. ROBERT R. BISHOP:

My dear Mr. President,— As I stated to you, I am unable to be present at the complimentary dinner to Mr. Gifford; but our Commonwealth will be represented by his Honor, the Lieutenant-Governor. I cannot forbear, however, to send my congratulations and express my respect for the veteran Clerk of the Senate, who has for a quarter of a century not only discharged the duties of his office, but endeared himself to a continually widening circle of friends. [Applause.]

Sincerely yours,

JOHN D. LONG.

I can echo what the Governor has said as to his endearing himself to his friends. For two years I sat by his side, and I must express what I have no doubt you all feel, that we are greatly indebted to him for his uniform kindness, and for the great pleasure with which he has attended to all our wants, and for his courtesy in all our intercourse in these many, many years. [Applause.]

I have now the pleasure of introducing to you the Lieutenant Governor of the State. [Applause.]

ADDRESS OF HON. BYRON WESTON.

Mr. President and Gentlemen,— It is with a great deal of diffidence that I rise before you to-night, and take the rôle

that has been assigned to me. I have figured as a
military man ; as a manufacturer ; like yourselves, in the
Senatorial capacity ; but, as a public speaker, especially
as one responding for the Commonwealth, my experience
is certainly very limited. You all remember the story
of the boy who said his father was a bank director, horse-
dealer, liquor-seller, and also a deacon ; but he did very little
business in the last line. [Laughter.] I can at least,
however, say that it does my heart good and awakens my
pride for the old Commonwealth to meet at this board so
many of the men who, during the last quarter of a century,
have occupied seats in the Senate of Massachusetts, some
of them as its presiding officers, one of them afterward the
Chief Magistrate of the Commonwealth, all representing
her enterprise and civilization. Especially am I glad to
pay my tribute of respect and of friendship to the faithful
Clerk, the genial companion, the wise and venerable head,
shining even brighter than the gilded dome under which
he serves, and almost as familiar to the people. [Laughter
and applause.] Where there are so many crowns upon
which this compliment would gracefully rest, perhaps it
is necessary to say I refer to our friend, the Hon. Stephen
N. Gifford. Where shall we look upon his like ? What
an eventful period of our history is spanned by his life !
Reaching from the days of the early Federalists even unto
the disappearing coat-tails of the *greenbacker*, and including
the triumphs of Webster, the overthrow of nullification,
the fervor of the anti-slavery movement, the struggles in
Kansas, the short-lived flash of Know-Nothingism, the
shining glory of John A. Andrew, the war and the triumph
of the nation against rebellion, and the happy return of the
grandest prosperity that ever shone upon a nation,—
Auditor, the father of the Senate, Clerk for twenty-five
years, the leading songster in the Senate choir of 1872
[laughter], not averse to the fisherman's rod, and the most
entertaining of conversationalists in his reminiscences of
the past ; well may the Commonwealth be called upon
to respond, when such a one of our public servants is

honored, and his long and faithful service recognized. I make no apology; for, had I the eloquence of all the orators, I could not represent Massachusetts better than by saying that she respects and honors Stephen N. Gifford, and trusts that he may serve her as long as he lives. [Applause.]

THE PRESIDENT.— Gentlemen, we have heard from the Commonwealth. I think it is about time we began to hear from our present Senators. We all know we have a presiding officer who has occupied the place for three years, having been in continuous service as a member of the Senate for five years, a remarkable thing nowadays; and we shall be glad to hear from him. We all honor and love him in his own home. No man is more popular in his city, the city of Newton, than Mr. Bishop, and I take great pleasure in introducing him.

Mr. Bishop was greeted with hearty and long continued applause; and, after it had subsided, he spoke as follows:—

ADDRESS OF HON. ROBERT R. BISHOP.

Mr. President,— I am sure that the reason why you call upon me is that I may have opportunity, on behalf of the present Senate, to express its sentiments of welcome and fellowship to its predecessors all along the line, on an occasion when we come together for the common purpose of tendering our united tribute of respect, of friendship, of recollection, and of love to the veteran Clerk of all these Senates, Stephen N. Gifford. [Applause.]

Any one who has read "Tom Brown's School Days at Rugby"—and every Senator is presumed to have read that book—will recollect that at all the reunions and anniversaries, when the students of many years come back, the day belongs to the old boys by right of a prior title, and the new boys are unceremoniously pushed aside. So, since I have not the slightest intention of admitting that I am an old boy, or that any one of my associates is such, we cheerfully grant, brethren of the former Senates, that the occasion is mainly yours,— that it is a time when the old precept should be observed that the younger portion of the family is to be seen and not heard [laughter]; and, grateful that it has been our good fortune to initiate this festival, we rejoicingly turn it over to your hands.

Welcome, then, Senators of the many Senates, to a revival, even though for one brief hour, of the recollections and the spirit of your former labors. Welcome again in spirit to the Senate Chamber, that grand old hall which Rufus Choate was accustomed to call "the finest legislative room in the world." It remains, in chaste dignity of appearance and in delightful cheerfulness, the same as when you left it. It is true the old fireplaces which flanked the President's desk have disappeared. It is true that the snuff-box which for generations ornamented one mantel-piece, and from which, as the most distinguished courtesy which he could bestow, the President took a pinch with strangers, has been carefully appropriated by the Secretary of State. [Laughter.] I am afraid that it is true that the old box of camomile flowers which graced the other will be found in the coat pocket of some one of the members of the Senate of 1858, Mr. Gifford's first Senate. [Renewed laughter.] But the drum and sword and Hessian cap and the guns are there. It is still the duty of the President, when the debates approach the dull and uninteresting point,—they never reach it [applause],— to gaze vacantly at the magnolia blossoms and the quaint festoons of oak leaves in the ceiling, and thus to give the appearance of being absorbed in rapt attention. [Laughter.] The desks of the law-makers are still there between the beautiful Corinthian pillars. The present Senate would never forgive me if I did not hasten to say that I do not mean in the slightest to imply that these are the only pillars of State which still remain. [Laughter and applause.] These are there, and you, fellow-Senators of the previous Senates, are there, in spirit. Call up the vivid, urgent, exigent debates and struggles of your time; when the tug and struggle was hard and sharp and long; when a single vote, it may be, carried or defeated measures which you, in your ardor, thought contained the remedy for all evils or carried the seeds of great ruin. How you fought over them! We are doing it all over again now. You are still there in your successors, fighting over again the battles which, to them, are equally urgent and pregnant, with equally varying fortune. How clearly, as one looks back, does the truth come out that it is not so much the success or failure of a specific measure which carries the marked consequences which you have apprehended, as it is that "out of the clashing of discordant views there comes the harmony of a perfect State." [Applause.]

These are all there, and — Mr. Gifford is there. He is there in the same quiet, unostentatious performance of the duties of his office, with the same urbanity and simplicity of manner, with the same clear sunlight shining through his character, with the same stability of manhood, as on the day when he first took the oath of office. [Applause.] Like the twelve tribes of Israel or the clans of the valley, we gather to-night, every one under its own banner; but our emotion toward him is described by the lines,—

> " Saxon and Norman and Dane are we,
> But all of us Danes in our welcome of thee."

How shall we speak of him as he deserves, and to his face? There is only one way in which a task at once so grateful and so delicate can be performed, and that is to speak as we feel, from the heart; and Mr. Gifford will pardon me, I am sure, if, in order to express my own feelings, which you all share, I repeat a conversation which I lately had with a friend of exquisite perceptions, about a portrait. Seeing a striking etching of Dean Stanley in his parlor, I said, "That's a strong face." "Yes," said he, "it is a strong face; but I always think that its strength comes from conviction and from conscience." My friends, Dean Stanley and Mr. Gifford are not relatives, so far as I know; but I ask you to look at that face on this memorial [holding up the portrait of Mr. Gifford upon the memento prepared for the guests], and, remembering that, in the long intercourse of years, no one of you ever heard him speak a word that you would wish unsaid, nor witnessed an act which did not increase your respect for his manhood, tell me if there is not something in your own feelings about its original that is stronger than friendship, higher than mere respect, deeper even than affection,— the conviction that his long life as a man and his quarter of a century as a public officer have been guided and governed by the highest behests of conviction and conscience, and not by will or personal purpose. [Applause.]

Speak of the perfect performance of his duties as Clerk of the Senate for this long period; speak of his absolutely incorruptible character and nature; speak of the great patience and kindness of his heart,— yet in our hearts to-night, over and above all other qualities,

> " His strength is as the strength of ten,
> Because his heart is clean."

[Great applause.]

THE PRESIDENT.— I think that approach to dulness in the speeches in the Senate, to which our excellent President has referred, must belong to the later generation. [Laughter.] We had a way of curing all such things in old times. We used to meet together, and remain about fifteen or twenty minutes; and then we had no difficulty with dulness, for we went over to the House, where it was lively.

The President has referred to the past Senates. A remarkable thing is this to-night that we have with us a President of the Senate who occupied the chair thirty-two years ago, who is now past eighty-four years of age, who is still in business, still a bank director, an insurance director, and whose voice is heard very often in different parts of the State. You all know to whom I refer; and I will, without further ado, introduce the Hon. Marshall P. Wilder.

At the announcement of the President, the entire company rose to their feet, and greeted Mr. Wilder with very hearty applause, who then spoke as follows :—

ADDRESS OF HON. MARSHALL P. WILDER.

Mr. President,—I am greatly obliged to you for your kind words, and to you, my good friends, for your cordial greetings on the announcement of my name. Yes, Mr. President, it is true, as you have intimated, that I am somewhat advanced in years; but, although I may have come down to you from a former century, I trust I shall never be so old as not to remember that I once held a seat in the Senate of Massachusetts [applause], or so ungrateful as not to appreciate highly the many other favors which have been conferred on me by my friends, during a long and protracted life. And now, Mr. President, I desire to return your compliment, and to say we owe you a debt of gratitude for the many valuable services which you have rendered to our city, State, and nation, and which we can never forget. [Applause.] Especially glad am I to meet again the distinguished President of the Senate, who so ably and gracefully discharges the duties of his high office, and by which great honor is conferred on our Commonwealth. [Renewed applause.] Mr. President, this is a special occasion; and I am most happy to be here and to participate with you and our friends in expressing our gratitude to our worthy guest for the long and valuable services he has rendered to our State. Few men have rendered more important or honorable service in her behalf. No one, since the organization of our government, has held the office which he now fills for so long a period; and I am sure, gentlemen, you will all unite with me in saying that no one has discharged the various duties thereof with more courtesy, fidelity, and ability. [Applause.] Long may he live to enjoy the confidence and esteem to which he is so justly entitled, and to occupy the same position, if he lives, for years to come. [Applause.] Mr. President, as you have alluded to my official relations with the Senate of Massachusetts in former years, and, standing here to-day as I do after an absence of thirty-two years from that body, I trust it may not be considered as out of place for me to refer for a moment to that time and some of the incidents of those days. That Senate, as now, was composed of forty members. Most of these have passed over the bridge of life. Only a few are left on this side of the river, and I alone am here to-night to tell the story of those days.

Among those that still live, I rejoice to number Henry L.
Dawes and William B. Washburn [applause], both of whom
have rendered most honorable services in behalf of our
State and nation, and whose names will be handed down to
posterity as benefactors of mankind. [Renewed applause.]
The session of 1850 was held in a time of great political
excitement, when the anti-slavery sentiment of New England was at its highest point. It was during that session
that Mr. Webster delivered his memorable 7th of March
speech in the Senate of the United States, a speech which
caused great discomfiture, even to some of his own friends.
So great was this that I may state to you, what is not gen-
erally known, that resolutions censuring him were presented
in that Senate ; but, thanks to a merciful Providence, after
Senators had slept over them for the night, they were with-
drawn, and thus that Senate escaped from a foul stain on its
records which would have disgraced it through all time.
[Applause.] Mr. Webster's speech was much misunderstood
and misrepresented at that time ; but let me say to you, gen,
tlemen, that I have read that speech over and over again-
have read it to-day, and I cannot, for my life, put my finger
on a single line but what is perfectly consistent with the
patriotism, loyalty, and integrity which characterized his
whole political life. But time sets all things right at last ;
and I think, if the public voice of to-day could be expressed,
it would be pronounced as one of the most self-sacrificing
and patriotic speeches of that immortal man, New England's
greatest son, America's most illustrious statesman. [Ap-
plause.] Mr. President, there are many distinguished gentlemen present who are to address this assembly, and I will
bring my remarks to a close. You will permit me, however,
to say again that I am very thankful to be here and to participate in the privileges and pleasures of this occasion, here
to meet so many old friends with some of whom I have been
acquainted for many years, here to exchange congratulations
on the continuance of our lives. It warms up the old heart,
the pulse beats stronger, the blood courses more freely in
my veins, and I live over again the life of former days.

[Applause.] But, gentlemen, I cannot disguise the fact that my days of pilgrimage on earth are nearly ended. I have long since passed the summit of the hill of life, and have descended down its western slope nearly to the sunset line; but, while life lasts, I shall never cease to thank the Giver of all good that he cast my lot in the midst of so many friends, and 'has permitted me to live for so long a time under the benign influence of those blessed principles which have made our nation what it is, the first great free and independent republic on earth, the strongest and best government in the world! [Loud applause.]

THE PRESIDENT.—The department of the government of Massachusetts in which the people have the most confidence, and to which they hold with extreme tenacity, is that of the judiciary. One of our Supreme Court judges has been placed upon the bench of the Supreme Court of the United States. His appointment gave pleasure and satisfaction throughout the nation. I do not think that the list is exhausted; and, if our President in his wisdom cannot find a judge to fill the place which is now vacant, he can come to Massachusetts again, and we can give him another man to fill it. [Applause.] I shall invite Judge Pitman to answer for himself in regard to that matter.

Judge Pitman was greeted with hearty applause, and spoke as follows : —

ADDRESS OF HON. ROBERT C. PITMAN.

Mr. President and Gentlemen,—I hardly know which startles me the most, the very flattering introduction, or the fact that I am brought into such close proximity to my venerable friend who has just addressed you. But, startling as it may be to be called on to address you next to the venerable ex-President Wilder, who rejoices in the age of eighty-four years, I suppose I am in my right place. For, of the Presidents of the Senate who come within the favored limit of twenty-five years covering Mr. Gifford's term of office, I stand next among the living to Governor Claflin.

Some special reminiscences are awakened when I recollect that the Presidents between Governor Claflin and myself have all departed. There is Governor Clifford, of glorious memory; there is President Field, honored for so many years; there is Joseph A. Pond, falling in the maturity of his powers; there is the genial friend of every man who was in the Senate, George Brastow; and I come next in order. I think, gentlemen, although I am not quite positive, in looking over the list, there are not more than nine living Presidents of the Senate, of whom we have six here to-night.

Dr. Johnson says, When there are a great many people, they come out of church slowly: when there are a few, they come out easily. So it is with ideas. When there is much crowding the mind, it is difficult to express it. I trust I shall not be slow; but, if you find a confusion of ideas, you must attribute it to the multiplicity of topics which crowd upon me.

One of the first thoughts that crowd upon my mind is, We have lost an anniversary; and this is an attempt, in part, to make up for the loss. A year and a half ago there was an anniversary which should have been memorable in every part of Massachusetts, it being then one hundred years since the Constitution of Massachusetts was adopted; and, though it is not actually so, it would seem that nobody in the Commonwealth of Massachusetts except our good Governor Long remembered that fact, and a few men who were gathered in the council chamber — and I esteem it an honor to have been one of them — to listen to the prayer of President Hopkins. That was all the celebration Massachusetts afforded of an accomplished fact so glorious as that, — one hundred years of freedom and prosperity under a constitution like the Constitution of Massachusetts. I do not know what possessed the Legislature of Massachusetts, — whether it was the shadow of General Butler in the distance to call them to account, if a few dollars were appropriated for that purpose. [Laughter and applause.] What a glorious opportunity to have gathered at the State House every living representative of every department of the government of Massachusetts (the number is not too large even for the House), and to have celebrated such an event as that! We have celebrated every skirmish, almost, in the war of the Revolution; but here is an event which goes beyond the end of the war, goes back even to the time when Massachusetts laid the foundations of her imperishable prosperity, and framed a constitution which no civilized government can surpass. But that opportunity has passed. It is something to gather the representatives for twenty-five years of even one department of the government.

Something has been said of the department of the government which I have the honor to represent, and perhaps I may be allowed to speak for the Superior Court. We have upon our bench now four who have been members of the Senate, and I think they will agree with me that a very valuable part of our training has come from the experience in making laws which we had there. Three other members of our court, making a majority of the whole, have seen service in the House. So you see that Massachusetts in her legislative halls trains men for all departments of her government. But I must differ from my worthy friend, whom I honor, as I ought, who presides here, in one or two matters. It would not be a Senate, if there were no difference and no debate. I wish to say to the Legislature of Massachusetts, and say without the bias of any personal feeling, that not only do I esteem your branch of the government the equal in honor and importance of any other branch of the government, but I say to you, Value your own position highly, respect yourselves, continue your sessions until you have finished the public business. [Applause.] Do not mind the cheap censures of the newspapers, or the snarling of your competitors whom you have distanced in the opinion of your fellow-citizens. [Applause.] Remember what Tennyson says, "Raw haste half-sister to delay." Hasty legislation results in doubt and confusion, as those who have to administer the laws ascertain. [Applause.]

But I am afraid I shall be borne away from the object of

the occasion. [Voices, "Go on!"] I know the sentiment of my excellent friend, the Clerk ; and I know that he will say " Amen " to what I have just expressed.

MR. GIFFORD.— Amen. [Loud laughter and applause.]

JUDGE PITMAN.— If I might venture to criticise my younger friends, I would say that it has been their fear that somebody would think they had better be in a hurry to close their session that has sometimes deteriorated their legisla- tion. I remember a few years ago calling the attention of the chairman of the judiciary of the House to the unconsti- tutionality of a law. The reply was, that it was too late in the session even to attend to the repeal of an unconstitutional law ; the consequence of which was that a brace of criminals soon afterward convicted of a felonious offence were dis- charged from the house of correction by a decision of the Supreme Court.

But, lest I forget and be driven from the subject by the modesty of my friend, I desire to say that, so ably and satis- factorily has he discharged the duties of his office during his long term of service, Mr. Gifford would have the vote of every Senator who has served during that time. I remember after I was elected President, in my confusion the first day, I put the vote in this form, "Senators in favor will say, 'Aye': those contrary-minded will say, 'No.'" I soon received a note, the handwriting of which I easily recog- nized, saying that Senators were not supposed to be contrary- minded. [Laughter and applause.] I think, if any Senator was to vote against a vote of thanks to Mr. Gifford, that Senator might well be called contrary-minded. [Renewed applause.]

Not only did Mr. Gifford never make an enemy, but he never said an unkind word. I never saw him when he was not as calm and unruffled as a morning in June,— that morn- ing in June, you know, that always foretells a pleasant and long day. And so I trust that the measure of his life will be so prolonged that he shall have that length of life that shall fully satisfy him. [Applause.]

THE PRESIDENT.— I trust my friend, the Judge, will pardon me if I suggest that the people sometimes think the Judiciary is not in a great hurry to decide their cases. [Laughter.] We have received from a former President of the Senate, my predecessor, a telegram, which I think should be read to you. It comes from Prague, in Austria : —

BISHOP, President of the Senate, Boston, Mass.: Heartiest, warmest greetings to friends of other days. CHARLES A. PHELPS.

I notice on my left a gentleman who has watched the clock very closely, as he intends to start soon for Washington ; and I have been even afraid that the railroad would take him in spite of us. Of all departments in the government which I might have said is least respected in Washington is the Agricultural [laughter]; the one that Senators and Representatives, remembering their constituents at home, and knowing that something ought to be done for the agricultural interests, are always ready to vote any amount of money for, though they would sneer privately, and sometimes publicly, about the uses made of it, such as raising tea in South Carolina, and bringing yachts from some other part of the globe to travel over the mountains with, and so on. But, finally, they came to Massachusetts to select a Commissioner of Agriculture, and they pitched upon exactly the right man. [Applause.] The whole country applauded as much as they did when Judge Gray was selected for the Supreme Court ; and I do not know that he will ever be able to get out of the office until he is removed to another sphere, judging from what we have seen since he has been in. But you know more about him than I do, and I know everything to his praise. He was with me in Congress four years, and always stood by me in every effort. We worked together and we lived together; and I cherish his friendship most heartily, as I know you do. I will not say further in his praise, but present to you the Hon. George B. Loring. [Loud applause.]

ADDRESS OF HON. GEORGE B. LORING.

Mr. President,— I certainly feel under great obligation
to you for the interesting, suggestive, and significant
introduction you have given me to my Senatorial friends
this evening, that I am just fitted to fill the most insignificant place in the government. [Laughter.] It is a
compliment so unusual, so rich, that I shall treasure it to
my dying day. [Renewed laughter.] I know now, sir,
just exactly what I am worth. I have never been able to
find out before during a long and useful life. [Laughter.]
I think, sir, you and I have escaped very well this evening.
I sit here among a class of gentlemen who have been
alluded to by the present President of the Senate as his
venerable predecessors; and he did it so gently and so
sweetly that I rather felt proud of my position here. I felt
I was fortunate to escape that appeal: "Venerable men,
you have come down to us from a former generation.
Heaven has bounteously lengthened out your life that you
may behold this joyous day." When I felt myself free
from that charge, and felt that there was one little spark
of youth remaining for Judge Pitman and myself, I
congratulated myself that I had been here, and shall return
to my duty with renewed energy, and endeavor to make
this most insignificant department of mine worthy of a
graduate of the Massachusetts Senate. [Applause.]

I have great respect for the Commonwealth of Massachusetts, and always had. I do not mean to say, situated
now as I am, that distance lends enchantment to the view;
for she certainly looks more charming and more delightful
when I am here than she possibly can at any distance.
Wherever I go, north, south, east, or west, I find the marks
and footsteps of the old Commonwealth so continually
that I am constantly reminded of the State of my birth;
more than that, I am reminded of the high service which
I have performed here in the State, and of the higher
service which my friends and associates have been enabled
to perform before me. Massachusetts has many institutions

of which she may well be proud. She has her Harvard
College, her Williams College, and other centres of learning
on every hand; and those of us who are graduates of those
schools feel proud of the position we have secured by our
associations. She has also her penitentiaries, which I do
not think it is a hardship to get into. [Laughter.] I
congratulate my fellow-citizens on the fact that no decree of
the judge who sits before me, and no jury, can send a man in
this State into an uncomfortable prison. [Laughter.] We
have our military organizations, which serve well in wars and
fight well in peace. We have our Hoosac Tunnel, the
model of all the great bores of this land [laughter], an
institution from which every graduate has gone forth
into the larger service of life, understanding exactly how
far public works can go and how far he can go in imposing
upon the good will of the American people. We have a
variety of institutions here, of which we are all proud. We
have our academies; and I see here and there, scattered in
this hall, graduates of those old schools who have never yet
forgotten the stern and painful discipline imposed upon
them in their early days by all these institutions in the
State of Massachusetts. And I defy any man in this land
to point to one more important, more significant, and whose
graduates have held higher honor than the Senate of the
State of Massachusetts. [Applause.]

I see here men who have distinguished themselves in
every walk in life, and who have graduated in that branch
of our government. Here, we have Governors, ex-Gov-
ernors, so called, who carried to their private homes all the
honors they have earned by their hard service in life, and
who, having served their State well, have upheld her
honor, her loyalty, and her glory on the battle-fields, and
have won for her additional renown in their service in the
great war for the Union. [Applause.] We have here
gentlemen who have done their service well everywhere.

When I went to Congress, I found myself surrounded by
Massachusetts Senators. I found in the Judiciary Committee one member, chairman of the Judiciary Committee in

the Massachusetts Senate when I was president. I waited a little while, and I found another one turning up on the Judiciary Committee; and it seemed as though Congress itself could not get along without the influence of the Massachusetts Senate. It was omnipresent. It seemed omnipotent. It was the great water-wheel that seemed to move the machinery of the national government.

Therefore, I think we have a right to be proud of the Senate of Massachusetts. When the State of Massachusetts was assailed in Congress, and I endeavored, in my humble way, to defend the old Commonwealth against the attacks that were made upon her suffrage policy, upon her loyalty in the late war, upon her position in history, the last fact that I stated that won the admiration and esteem of the House of Representatives was this: when the Senate of Massachusetts passes into the chamber where its deliberations are conducted, it passes beneath the drum that beat the reveille, and the musket that blazed in the line, when the power of the Anglo-Saxon was established on this continent, and the American flag was carried far on beyond the waters of the Labradors, almost to the frozen seas. [Applause.] The last thing that won their esteem, and put the old Commonwealth where she should be, was the fact that the Senate of Massachusetts assembled under those circumstances. I did not say anything about the House. [Laughter.] I did not say anything about the Council. I said we had good and righteous judges; and they who opposed us said, "We have good and righteous judges." I said, "We have an able Executive"; and they said, "So have we." But, when I began to beat that old drum, and fire off the old gun, down they came [applause]; and they wished they had such a drum and such a gun. And I said, "You will, if you live long enough." Longevity is a great thing in this world. I am happy to see that some Senators in the Senate of Massachusetts seem determined to follow in the same path.

I think the Senate of Massachusetts is a convenient body to belong to. There are just enough members to be sociable, just enough to make a noise, just enough to have trouble in, and just enough to quiet the whole trouble, and come out in a dignified and proper manner. Tell me, if the House of the last twenty-five years could get up such a dinner as this [laughter], such an assembly as this. Why, this hall would be crowded and overrun by the ambitious young statesmen that have served this Commonwealth so well. Call together the membership of the Council of this State for the last twenty-five years, and there would not be enough to fill one table; but, when you come to the Senate, whose number was fixed to forty members by the Constitutional Convention in 1820, when Mr. Webster said there were so few men in the State that had any money it must be small, and consequently they fixed the number at forty, it certainly is the most convenient, most admirable, most successful number ever heard of. [Applause.] You can tie forty,— you cannot tie forty-one!

Now, in the midst of all the successful endeavors of the Senate of Massachusetts, we have had a Clerk here for twenty-five years; and I am not at all sorry that the Senators who have served with him were anxious to take advantage of this anniversary of his, and come together in kindly accord around the festive board. Why, he has set us a good example in all good feeling. He is an amiable gentleman. He makes no quarrels with anybody, and keeps himself always in condition to dine with the Senators on all occasions. So far as I know, he is an admirable example in that respect, so that, as a social gentleman, he is the model Clerk of the Massachusetts Senate. He brought into the Senate of Massachusetts twenty-five years ago the spirit of the old colony from whence he came; and I have no doubt the courage of Miles Standish has been coursing in his veins from that day to this, and I can see that the beauty of Priscilla Mullins is in his face. [Laughter and applause.] I know that he has been true to the doctrines that were established at Plymouth by the Pilgrims of 1620. I am sure that, in all his devotion to principle, he has manifested a resolution and determination which he got

nowhere else but on that sacred spot. Did you ever know
him to waver, when I have appealed to him to know
whether, in resisting the claims of the House in regard
to originating bills, the Senate was in the right? I never
knew him to say the House was in the right. [Applause.]
I never knew a man so loyal. Why, he would always stand
by us ; and, when the Senators were called into the House
in convention assembled, with what an air of magnificent
triumph he has led the way for the President and his
followers, as if to say, " Here we are : see what a dignified
body of gentlemen we are." [Laughter.] I do not wonder
the Senators all love him, and desire to have him continue
in office as long as he lives ; and I agree with them that
a more thoroughly model Clerk has never been known in
the Massachusetts Senate. I am sure that, as time goes on,
he will find, if he desires to find it, that he is entitled to
that benediction (I do not know that he desires it, I do not
know that he has ever contemplated the end, or ever will
[laughter], I do not ask him to), but, when he does, I remind
him, he is perfectly entitled to the benediction, " Mark the
perfect man, and behold the upright ; for the end of that
man is peace." [Loud applause.]

THE PRESIDENT.— See what a secretary agriculture will
have, when the department is brought into the Cabinet.
[Applause.] The oldest of the former Presidents of the
Senate now living is the Hon. Josiah Quincy. He was
invited to be present with us this evening, and we were
in some hopes he would be here ; but he has finally determined, although in good health, that his great age will not
permit him. We all know his service to the Commonwealth
in past time, what he did for the Western railroad and for
many other enterprises ; and we honor him. Those who
know him best esteem him most highly. As he is the
oldest of former Presidents, and cannot be with us, it is my
pleasure to introduce to you one of the younger, who has
filled the chair of President with great acceptance and with
great eloquence. I have now the pleasure of introducing

without further words the Hon. Horace H. Coolidge. [Applause.]

ADDRESS OF HON. HORACE H. COOLIDGE.

Mr. President,— It has been my fortune many times to attend public dinners in honor of those who have served their country well. Sometimes, I have spoken; but upon no occasion have I been called upon to do so, when I have responded with so earnest a feeling as comes now from my heart in honoring the guest of this evening. It has been given me to have been associated with him officially perhaps a longer number of years than any gentleman now present. I entered the House in 1865, and remained there three years, and from the committees on which I served learned then to know the Clerk of the Senate. In 1869, I entered the Senate; and no one received me more cordially than the Clerk. In 1870, I was chosen to the Presidency, and here let me give a little incident. Prior to the assembling of the Senate,— the night before, indeed,— a caucus of the whole Senate was called. By their kindness, I was unanimously nominated; but I remember that a Senator, so much and so truly regretted by me and all who knew him, the Hon. Ellis W. Morton, got up and said that for the benefit of the new Senators he would state that the Senate of Massachusetts could never be properly organized without the unanimous nomination of Stephen N. Gifford, as Clerk. [Applause.] The whole Senate agreed with him, and the thing was done. From that day to this,— yes, and for years before,— that verdict was always given. And why? Because Massachusetts is an honest State. God bless her! And Gifford has shown himself, for twenty-five years, an honest officer, an honest patron, and an honest man. Is there more to ask for in this grand old Commonwealth? Let me say to you all, my friends, who have assembled to do honor to our beloved guest, that not one of you can so appreciate and love him as those of us who have sat in the chair of the Senate, and who know, as no others can, our obligations to him, so modestly and so simply rendered, and yet always with a learning and devotion to his branch of the General Court which could not but impress us each and all. I cannot conclude without alluding to one trait in our dear friend's character that impressed me more than all. He is, was, and always will be, as I most earnestly hope, a man of most pronounced convictions upon every subject, political or otherwise. And yet no man who has ever met him during his whole twenty-five years of service can say that he ever attempted to interfere unduly with legislation. On the contrary, I had the opportunity for three years, as President, to watch the patience with which he listened to every man who came to that desk of his, so open to interruption that it would have driven many of us wild, never ruffled, always ready to answer all questions, knowing well that all those interruptions would cost him half a night of sleep, yet always the same calm gentleman you see him now. Do we not do ourselves good this night to honor him, the simple, modest gentleman who has done so much for us ; and am I not right in applying to him these words of Tennyson? —

> " For who can always act? but he
> To whom a thousand memories call,
> Not being less, but more than all
> The gentleness he seemed to be,
>
> " Best seemed the thing he was, and join'd
> Each office of the social hour
> To noble manners, as the flower
> And native growth of noble mind;
>
> " Nor ever narrowness or spite,
> Or villain fancy fleeting by,
> Drew in the expression of an eye.
> When God and Nature met in light;
>
> " And thus he bore without abuse
> The grand old name of gentleman,
> Defamed by every charlatan
> And soiled with all ignoble use."

[Applause.]

THE PRESIDENT.— I am reminded that the time is passing on, and some of you may be obliged to leave. Our friend, the guest of the evening, has been working his way down the list as far as he can; but I shall not let him go any longer, and therefore I shall present to you Stephen N. Gifford, Clerk of the Senate.

As Mr. Gifford rose in response to the introduction by the President, he was greeted with hearty cheers and applause, the entire company rising on their feet. When the applause had subsided, Mr. Gifford said : —

ADDRESS OF STEPHEN N. GIFFORD.

I think, friends, if anybody had said to me this morning that there were as many men in the State of Massachusetts who had ever been my constituents as are here present, I never would have believed it; and I know that there are not the same number of good-looking men in the United States. [Applause.]

There is only one man that I have any spite against here, and I want to free my mind in regard to him for this reason. In one of his valedictory addresses, he alluded to me as "the venerable Clerk of the Senate." I looked in the register, and I found that he was just two years younger than I. [Laughter.] Now, I did not like it. Still, I am old enough : there is no doubt about that. [Applause.]

But I think I may say it would require a more eloquent tongue than mine fitly to respond to the many kind things that have been said here to-night. I feel as if I had been travelling in some far-off land, and, after years of absence, had returned to my friends once more; and, as I meet the old familiar faces, I see the same genial smile, I hear the same kindly greeting, I feel the same hearty shake of the hand of days long ago. I look around for other familiar faces, and I find them not; but instead, in my mind's eye, I see a long, long procession passing down the dark valley and beyond that bourne whence no traveller returns. In that procession, I see men who sat by your side, men who worked shoulder to shoulder with you for the honor of the old Commonwealth, men who devoted their best energies to make their native State a model Commonwealth, to make her what she is, the Queen of New England. In that procession, I see a Clifford, the jurist, the Governor, your President, Wentworth of Middlesex, Bailey of Fitchburg, second to no man in ability in the County of Worcester,—"he was my friend, faithful and just to me,"—Pond of Middlesex, a born presiding officer, Brastow of Middlesex, Field of Berkshire, Loring of Suffolk, who was unimpeachable on a question of law. And then there was that Bayard of Suffolk, young Morton, a man without fear and without reproach, than whom no man ever had a brighter future, had not disease marked him for its own. He faltered, died, and, like Milton's Lycidas, he was dead ere his prime ; and, to those who bore him to his grave, no fitter words could be said than those of the poet, "Tread lightly, comrades, for 'tis a man ye bear."

Those who knew him will fully appreciate what I have said; and the pleasing memories that cluster round the names of those men that were here, men that we saw every day, will still remain. It is a sad reflection, and humiliating as well, that every day's experience teaches us that it matters not how exalted a position a man holds, no matter how many vast enterprises seem to rest on his shoulders, bound up in the issues of his life, the existence of a nation depending on his presence in its councils,—the summons comes, he falls, and is gone, and the words, "The king is dead ! Long live the king !" are as true to-day as when said in ancient times. The ranks close up. "Some short bustle is caused, a few inquiries, and the solemn brood of care plod on." But it must be so. Yet, the world's work must be done. We must do it. "Duty exists, immutably survives." Gentlemen, twenty-five years is a long time in a man's life. A man is fortunate to have lived that time in active life, more fortunate to have lived those years in Massachusetts, still more to have lived that time in the United States. Twenty-five years ago, we heard the mutterings of the tempest which was soon to burst with relentless fury upon our nation. For four long years, we saw the spectacle of what the immortal

Webster so feared,— States dissevered, discordant, belliger-
ent; but, with the ability of our statesmen and by the
strong arms of the Boys in Blue, the old flag once more
floats over a *United* States, not a star erased nor a stripe
polluted, bearing on all its shining folds those glorious words
in their fullest meaning, " All men are created equal; liberty and union, one and forever, inseparable."

I believe any man who takes public office, takes it for the
accommodation of the public, not to accommodate himself
[applause]; and I believe, further, that, when there is any
thing to do, he should go and do it and say as little about it
as possible. [Applause.] Every man in office may have
cause for irritation. Every man who has ever held a public
office, and especially the one which I have had the honor to
hold so long, fully realizes the trouble and interruption that
he is continually experiencing; but the first quality for any
man in public office is that of a gentleman [applause], and
the quality of a gentleman is of very much the same quality
as that which Shakspere speaks of in regard to mercy, " It
blesses him that gives and him that takes." It has a reflex
action which gives a man the possession of his own faculties.

Then, as to good humor, I think that is one of the abso-
lute essentials for a public officer. If a man is to be irritated
by any little interruption, I think the best thing he can do is
to resign at once. [Laughter and applause.] That, perhaps,
may explain my idea of the administration of the duty of a
public office.

Perhaps I may speak of the legislative department, having been connected with it for a *short* time; although, during
the twenty-five years that I have been in the Senate Chamber, I have never been asked until to-night to make a speech.
[Loud laughter.] Well, now, I have seen the time when I
would like to do it [renewed laughter]; and I can tell you
one thing, that three years ago, if I had been asked to make
a speech, I think the salary bill would have been tremen-
dously afflicted. However, I did not have the opportunity.

But there is one thing I would like to say in vindication of
the General Court of Massachusetts. The constitution au-

thorizes the voters of this Commonwealth to meet on a given
day and choose Representatives and Senators to the Legislature of Massachusetts. Well, the people go to work, and
sometimes have a very hard fight; but the result is, taking
all things into consideration, they elect what they believe to
be the best men. They sometimes make a mistake. Every-
body does. [Uproarious laughter.] But the Legislature is
not in session more than a week, when you will see in the
papers, or hear some man say: "What are those men doing?
They have been there a week, and have not passed a bill yet."
So it goes on; and, in the course of a month, you will hear
it said, "Of course, they went up there to get the money;
and I suppose they will stay there until they think they can
make more money elsewhere, and then they will go home."
And when the first dandelion appears above the grass in the
State House yard, there comes a howl at the long session of
the Legislature; and if there is a poor robin whistling in the
leafless elm on the Common [laughter], no matter if he is
whistling to keep his courage up, it makes no difference,—
"It is about time for them to go home."

Now, there are some things of importance in the history
of Massachusetts; and I want to know to what the character of the Commonwealth is due but to her General
Court. Look at her schools; look at her public institutions;
look at her charitable institutions. Who framed the Acts
under which they rose? Who made provision for their sup-
port? Who has made Massachusetts the best commonwealth on the face of God's earth but the Legislature of
Massachusetts? [Applause.] No other power can do it;
and I say that the character of Massachusetts here and
everywhere where she is known, is due to the honesty, the
fidelity, the industry of the General Court [renewed ap-
plause]; and I say further, and I know whereof I affirm, that
the members of the Legislature of Massachusetts, those
who manage the business, work harder, work more hours,
than they would in their own business at home. I say further—and I can say that, because I have no fear of contradiction—they work a good deal harder than I would.

[Laughter.] I say it is unjust; and, if the people understood it, they never would be a party to this tirade.

Gentlemen, I thank you. If there were any words stronger than these, I would use them. I most respectfully thank you for all your kindness, for the unvarying kindness of every member of the Senate with whom I have been acquainted. I have this pleasant recollection that I never knew a member of the Senate to leave it with a feeling of enmity toward myself.

When Mr. Gifford concluded his address, the company again rose to their feet, and cheered and applauded their honored and honorable friend.

THE PRESIDENT.— Gentlemen, I suppose that you have observed that our friend the Clerk has a poetical nature and loves poetry. It would hardly answer in such an assembly as this not to have some one who could give us some lines in a different strain from that most of us are accustomed to use. I am very happy to say that one of the Senators of former years is present with us, and I presume will favor us with some of his poetry, Hon. Henry S. Washburn.

POEM BY HENRY S. WASHBURN.

Ho! comrades, why this gathering of old friends tried and true?
What service has the Commonwealth for you and me to do?
'Twas long ago we shook the dust from off our parting feet,
And yet as Senators once more we now together meet.
The fair dome of the Capitol looms grandly on our sight;
And Boston holds the whole of us in her embrace to-night.

We thought we framed enough of laws to last the State for years,—
That we could not her future know, now very plain appears;
For, ever more the people come with wants to be supplied,
With projects for the public good which may not be denied.

But why this gathering to-night? the Muse again inquires,
For brightly on the old hearthstone burn newly kindled fires;
And we are waiting for the Clerk the Senate roll to call,
To send the answer back, " We're here," for duty, one and all.

No, no, not all! We miss, alas! some of our foremost men,
Who bravely acted well their part with ready voice and pen;

The earnest soul and eloquent who with us, hand in hand,
Pressed on, until his footsteps passed the unknown border-land.

Yet one remains who faithfully, through long, unbroken years,
Has kept a record of our words which fell upon his ears ;
A sentinel with less of frown than humor in his eyes,
Who still the oil for Senate lamps abundantly supplies ;
Our honored guest, who to his post still clings through rain and shine,
The model of all clerks who've served in that distinguished line.

We come to pay the tribute which his silvered locks inspire ;
To tell him how we prize him as his days of life expire ;
To take him once more by the hand and wish him still God-speed,
Who o'er and o'er has been to us a helpful friend indeed.
He knows how, when we blundered, he hastened to our aid,
And by his tact how oft we have a decent record made :
How when, perchance, the President a moment left the chair,
Through him we have been able a good point to declare.
So quietly he moved about, the Chamber never knew
His was the merit of the act which its attention drew.

'Tis said our friend who, modestly, hath this distinction won,
Has features which resemble much the face of Washington,—
An honor any man might prize ; and 'tis his rightful claim
No action of his life has been unworthy of that name.

O brothers ! 'tis no easy task to fill so fair a page,
And hold a place of public trust almost from youth to age ;
To win respect, and bear away the love of friend and foe,
And leave fresh garlands strewn along our pathway as we go.
Such is his due whose brow to-night with laurels we entwine,
Our record at this festive board,— your offering and mine.

But brief our lay ; yet we would fain, ere this glad hour is o'er,
A blessing breathe for our good State we never honored more.
Her influence, carping critics claim, is on the wane to-day ;
That her prestige, once potential, is vanishing away ;
That mightier States are rising, nearer the setting sun,
Which will eclipse the glory in her early days she won,
When her Adamses and Quincys with right o'er might prevailed,
And foes of human liberty before their presence quailed.

Believe it not.   List ! even now, I hear her old-time cry,
"'A man's a man for all of that !' gainsay it we defy ;
And upon our boundless acres, where weary feet may tread,
There's room enough for all to come and earn their daily bread."

So, echoing long this pæan, we part for hearth and home;
Again, as we have gathered now, we nevermore may come.
But this shall be our glory: should the nation need a soul,
Whose strong arm will be able her future to control,
Right here will rise a Webster, an Andrew, or a Long,
To steer the good Ship safely through anarchy and wrong.

[Applause.]

THE PRESIDENT.— Many years ago, it was my fortune to be elected when a young man to the Legislature. I took my seat in the House with three hundred others; among them, a young man whom I had heard of before, from Waltham. His name at that time had even filled the Commonwealth; and he came into the House with just expectations, and those expectations have been most honorably and gloriously fulfilled. After having the highest honors of the State, after serving his country on the field, after having had honors in the House of Representatives in Congress, he has returned to Massachusetts and been a Senator; and it is my great pleasure to welcome him here to-night, as you all do. I have now the pleasure of introducing to you Hon. N. P. Banks.

General Banks was greeted with three cheers, the assembly rising to do him honor.

ADDRESS OF HON. N. P. BANKS.

Mr. President,— Were not your commands laid so heavily upon me at the commencement of the pleasures of the evening, I certainly should not trespass upon the patience of the company to-night; but I am very grateful for the opportunity of being present, of looking upon the company by which I am surrounded, and of listening to the sentiments of the gentlemen who have spoken so eloquently and so truthfully as well as beautifully.

I came here like you, Mr. President, and the rest of you, gentlemen, to honor my friend, Mr. Gifford, whom I have known a long time,— not exactly in the way and with the zest and right which you have to honor him in his position as Secretary of the Senate, but still to give him my meed of praise as well as I can. I will, however, speak rather of the office which he holds than of the manner in which he has discharged its duties; for I can add nothing to that which has been said, nor do I think anybody else can.

The office of secretary of a body like the Senate, or of a secretary anywhere, though lowly in character, and often-times in disesteem by the masses of the people, is every-where and always a post of great responsibility, requiring the highest qualities of intellect and of heart, depending more upon the integrity of the man that fills it than almost any other office that has been held. I could give, sir, one or two illustrations of this which would justify the high praise which gentlemen have given our friend who is here to-night. M. Thiers, in his history of the Empire of France, at the close of that contest which overthrew the first emperor, Napoleon, a man who thought he might with becoming modesty count himself as the third among the great men who had been created to rule the destinies of the world, and who, I think, might very well be counted among the first in that great contest which overthrew the first Napoleon and destroyed the empire,— the historian mentions an honorable thing in the performance of his task, attributes the success of that final campaign to an unknown man without fortune or influence or power, who was the secretary of the first Alexander of Russia. In my own time, in one of the most important contests of our day, which perhaps enlisted the interest of the people of this country more than any other contest in the last third or half of a century even, which has been of some importance in its influence upon the destiny of the country since that time, I saw a man for nine weeks to an hour who held in his hand at any moment the power to close that contest against the majority who finally won a triumph, and who had every temptation held out to him to use his power, and yet who, faithful to his trust, left it to be decided according to the wishes and according to the votes of those to whom by the Constitution it was delegated. If that man had failed to be in his place at any moment on any morning, the contest would have been over ; but he never failed. The tick of the clock found him at his place ; and thus was decided one of the great contests, one of the important contests of this country. And the name of the man is entitled to the respect of the people of this country, when I speak of the Clerk of the House of Representatives in 1855 and 1856,— an office occupied by John W. Forney, of Pennsylvania.

There is scarcely an administration anywhere that does not rely largely upon the secretary,— Great Britain upon the Secretary of the Queen, and the European governments upon their Secretaries. Who is it that directs the destinies of this country ? The Secretary. The greatest capacity, the highest possible attainments, the strictest integrity, are required for an office like this. Such is the character our friend possesses. I will not add to the qualifications, lest some unsophisticated persons might think hereafter that such an office, filled by such a man as Gifford, might enable the people of the Commonwealth to get along another quarter of a century without any Senators at all. [Applause.]

But, sir, I am reminded, when I look around upon those whom I ought to have known better, that I have been much absent from this State for a long period of time, and that I see now before me, I may say without extravagance, the Representatives of the people that have, in the last quarter of a century, made Massachusetts what it is, who have enabled her to influence the destinies of the country to the extent and in the manner in which she has done ; that is, they are Representatives in one branch of her Legislature which has given her her renown, as well as her influence and power, and has bestowed upon the country that meed of success which we have attained in the contests which we have had. As such, Mr. President, I salute these gentlemen, and as such I honor them. I can remember myself when I thought the Senate of Massachusetts was not a very lively place. I have heard people oftentimes speak lightly of it : very frequently, they are inclined to speak lightly of public men [laughter] ; but at one time, by some accident or other, I was chosen to a seat in the Senate of Massachusetts, and

I served for several months as a member of that Senate ; and I am prepared to say, sir, that in my time I have seen many parliamentary assemblies, I have assisted in the business of many sessions of legislative bodies, I know pretty well their history and their character and the influence which they have borne upon the affairs of this country, and, while I have been perhaps unduly careless of my part in them, so far as I have been connected with them, I never have forgotten what has been transacted before my eyes. And I remember distinctly my career and my experience in this regard ; and yet I take pleasure in saying that, with regard to the variety of the interests discussed, the novelty of questions, the power brought into the discussion of these questions in the Senate of Massachusetts, where, in 1874, I was a member, that I would be better pleased to have preserved my record in that session than any other part of my life. I should feel more secure and more satisfied with my public service in that record as Senator from the Second Middlesex District in 1874, as much so at least as any other part of my public life ; and I appreciate, therefore, from my experience, the truth of much that has been said by gentlemen in regard to that service.

One reason of this is that in the Senate of Massachusetts legislative debate is exactly what it should be,—directed to the question, discussed by men who have made themselves acquainted with its merits, who know by experience what has been done in the past, and by good judgment what should be done in the future, and thus bring to every question that is adopted and decided in this body to which we have all referred a judgment as perfect as man can bring to the decision of any public legislation. I have seen many assemblies of this character elsewhere, I have taken part in many legislative sessions, and I have never known any place where debate has been so exactly what legislative debate should be as in the Senate of Massachusetts ; and I am happy, sir, to have had the opportunity of saying thus much. Our influence upon our country, and to some extent upon the world itself, has been moulded and has been produced by legislation of this character, and by the services of public men of the character I have described; and I trust the Legislature of Massachusetts will hereafter continue in the hands of the same class of men, and be directed to the same great interests of liberty and justice, until the principles of the legislation of this State shall prevail in every part of the world, and characterize and bless the people of every portion of the earth. [Applause.]

THE PRESIDENT.— We have one with us who has been an honor to the State by his clear decisions and straightforward character. I have the pleasure of now presenting to you Speaker Noyes, of the House. [Applause.]

ADDRESS OF HON. CHARLES J. NOYES.

Mr. President,— At such a time and in such a presence as this, any one may rise with reluctance to respond for any body in which he had the honor of a seat; and more especially might he hesitate to speak, following the distinguished gentlemen who have already addressed those present, whose bright, shining sickles never leave anything to be gleaned by those who follow in their rear.

Looking back, Mr. President, over the mists of fifteen years, recalling the honored names of my associates in the Senate of 1867, I might well hesitate and feel grieved that this task had not fallen to abler hands than mine. I remember very well the brief experience I had in the Senatorial branch of the government. I remember the honored names of my associates, who have added very much to the glory and reputation of this good old Commonwealth. I remember the sad duty that Senate had to perform of following to his honored but untimely grave the distinguished gentleman who presided over our deliberations, whose grace, whose dignity, whose handsome presence no member of the Senate of 1866 can live long enough to forget, a man whose loss this Commonwealth might well lament for all time to come,— Hon. Joseph A. Pond. And I remember at his right hand sat the warm-hearted, the genial, and accomplished gentleman, who afterward was called to be a successor in his office; and upon his left, a gentleman, who to-day, in the advanced years of his life, still holds undisputed sway upon the floor of the popular assembly of the Legislature. I remember the distinguished merchant of Springfield, Mr. Alexander, and all the other associates; but time fails me to repeat their names, who at that time served with distinction, and have added new laurels as the years have gone on to the glory they then acquired. That Senate is a matter of the past. Its conflicts have ended, the tumult of its voices is silent; but, however so much, Mr. President, we may have disagreed upon other questions, we always cordially agreed in extending our esteem, our grateful recognition, and our heart-felt thanks to the genial, the companionable, and assisting Clerk, who did so much for our comfort and our convenience in promoting the public business of that year. [Applause.] It has been truly said, it seems to me, that, "though the head may whiten, the heart keeps young and fresh." And so it is with Mr. Gifford. I cannot help comparing him to that scene the traveller finds among the Alps,— when the glaciers glitter overhead, beneath are the wild flowers, blooming sweetly in the spring, scattering their fragrance on the frosty air. [Applause.]

So, Mr. President, while I regret that the duty of speaking for the Senate of 1867 has not been committed to the charge of a much abler person, I am yet happy to come here to-night in a humble way to add my felicitations to yours and my associates at this table, and to assist in rendering the esteem and honor which Mr. Gifford deserves from every man who ever had occasion to have official relations with him in public life. And so, with tearful remembrance of the dead and kindliest esteem for the living, I bring to him to-night the good words that would be spoken by lips that are silent had they the power, and the kindly words that would be brought here by the living who are absent; and, should he call the roll of the Senate of 1867, every one would vote, "Yea," in honor of him. [Applause.]

THE PRESIDENT.— It is now time that we heard from the western part of the State. We always hear good news from the Connecticut Valley. Among the honored names from that part of the State is one who served in the Senate, who has been offered higher positions, and yet, with a modesty peculiar to him, he has refused them,— not even allowing himself to be sent to Congress, which is a remarkable thing. We shall be very glad to hear from him. We recognize the fact that there are two parties in the Senate, though I do not hear anything of them in your speeches. We shall be very glad to hear from the Hon. George M. Stearns, of Chicopee. [Applause.]

ADDRESS OF HON. GEORGE M. STEARNS.

Mr. President,— I am very happy indeed you have called upon me to-night ; for I am very glad of the opportunity to bring my chaplet, even though it be of modest river roses and daisies, and lay it at the feet of our honored guest. I am also happy on my own account. I am glad to be able even for a fleeting moment to rescue from the shadow of forgetfulness the fact that I, too, have been a Senator of Massachusetts. [Applause.] During the "late unpleasantness" between the two sections of this country, as Major of the Home Guards [laughter] I so brilliantly conducted the prudent art of self-defence by the avoidance of danger [renewed laughter] that, at the close of the war, I was swept by a grateful people upon the waves of military popularity into the Senate Chamber [laughter and applause] ; and ever since that time, like many another martial hero, my name and fame have been folded beneath oblivion's dusky wave. [Laughter.]

In 1871, I came to the Massachusetts Senate with the average qualifications of a Massachusetts Senator; that is to say, I knew nothing of my duties or the method of their performance. [Applause and laughter.] I joined with those in the Senate in like situation, and we constituted a majority of the number. [Renewed laughter.] Of course, under these circumstances, we resorted to the Clerk. We beleaguered his leisure, we invaded his privacy, we intruded upon his quiet, we interrupted his labor, we smote his ears with questions, we besieged his private working-room, we overturned his spittoon, we gobbled his snuff, we took his fragrant Havanas, manufactured from Suffield seconds. [Laughter.] But, during all this, we found the same obliging, generous, genial, patient, pleasant Clerk that many a Massachusetts Senator had found before, and many a Massachusetts Senator has found since.

Nature never deceives. She makes the ceaseless murmur of the sea and tossing foam declare the rocks beneath the waters ; and so she always surmounts an honest heart with a noble face. I recollect at one time, as Clerk Gifford sat at his desk overlooking his charge with a benign gaze, his countenance illuminated with the light within, that I noticed a Democratic brother of mine at the Senate bar who sat watching, with worshipful wonder, the transfigured Clerk. Chancing at that time to desire to make a quotation in a speech I was about to make, I turned to Senator Parks, of Suffolk, who was the acknowledged authority in the Senate upon all Scriptural matters [laughter], and I said to him, "Bill, who composed the Lord's prayer?" [Laughter.] "Why," says he, "Gifford." [Loud and uproarious laughter.] Says I, "That can't be so : he is not so old as that, is he?" [Renewed laughter.] But I saw from the look he gave me that his faith and trust were so deep and implicit that they were not to be shaken, even by the contradiction of one of the unterrified faith. So I left him, and abandoned the fruitless endeavor.

Mr. President, I am happy to say that the retrospect that our friend Gifford has is one that is rarely granted to man, — twenty-five years of public service without a stain ; twenty-five years of association with six hundred exacting Senators without a jar ; twenty-five years of public labors without a mistake ! Long may the Commonwealth be spared the able head, the honest heart, and the indefatigable hand of the Senate Clerk. [Applause.]

THE PRESIDENT.— Gentlemen, I have succeeded so well in going to the valleys, I think I will try again, and seek a man from the valley of the Merrimack, one who comes from the city of Lawrence, and which the gentleman has made famous,— Mr. Tarbox, who is known all through the land. [Applause.]

ADDRESS OF HON. JOHN K. TARBOX.

Mr. President,— Did I essay to speak the praises of our guest, I could but iterate what has been already most fitly and gracefully spoken. This distinguished and representative company met to grace his public service with their approbation is the occasion's best orator. For a quarter of a century, the recorder, by annual election, of the transactions of the most dignified legislative body of the State, approved for integrity, capacity, and the agreeable qualities which win esteem by the judgment of twenty-five successive Senates, Mr. Gifford can need no fairer testimonial of the acceptability of his labors. Although, during that period, the political party of his sympathies has controlled the Senate organization, yet we here can testify with unanimous voice that his repeated election has not been due to partisan favor or in payment of partisan services, or to any servility on his part, but to a just estimate of his worth as a man and official. That Massachusetts delights to honor such as he in her places of trust is creditable to our good Commonwealth ; and I am sure I may command all your voices in the sentiment that, if the same test and spirit of selection obtained in all the departments of public administration, there would exist no such occasion as now unfortunately does exist for people and statesmen to agitate the evils and needs and methods of reform in the civil service. We do well and worthily, I think, sir, to bestow our plaudits generously in praise and encouragement of conscientious fidelity in our public servants at a season when the decadence of the nice sense of duty and responsibility in public trusts excites general solicitude.

One quality of Mr. Gifford, displayed in my intercourse

with him while a member of the Senate, I recall with agreeable sensibility. He never made me feel the ignominy of my disreputable politics. [Laughter.] Whatever his thoughts were, he considerately kept them to himself, and used me as fairly and courteously as though I were a good Republican and a veritable man and brother. [Renewed laughter.] Indeed, for aught I was able to discover, he served me as acceptably in that relation as would even a fellow-disciple of the faith of our Democratic apostle, Jefferson. That kindly memory, sir, and the gracious atmosphere of this delightful political truce, inspire in me the sentiment which I venture to express, that the asperities of our politics may soften and yield to a broader tolerance and a larger charity, and our party contentions dignify into a patriotic emulation as to which can worthiest serve the common welfare and advance the reputation of our State and the beneficence of the Republic. [Applause.] I heartily unite with this goodly company in wishing Mr. Gifford continued length of happy life and useful public service. [Applause.]

In the temporary absence of the President of the evening, Hon. Robert R. Bishop, who had taken the chair, called upon the Hon. J. M. S. Williams, of Cambridge, as a distinguished member of the Senate, and a gentleman who had rendered important service in the public affairs of the country.

ADDRESS OF HON. J. M. S. WILLIAMS.

I join in all that has been said, Mr. President, in regard to Mr. Gifford, and my association with him in the Senate will ever be pleasant to remember; but I will not occupy time at this late hour of the evening.

Mr. Bishop.— Gentlemen, allow me to call upon Mr. Fuller, of Westfield, a member of the Senate whom I very well remember when I was myself a member of the House of Representatives.

ADDRESS OF HON. HENRY FULLER.

Mr. President,— I had supposed the speakers of the even-ing had all been selected. I cannot make any extended remarks here this evening. I can only add to what has been said in behalf of my friend, Mr. Gifford, with whom I had the pleasure to serve three years, 1868, 1874, and 1875, that he was always the courteous gentleman that he has been represented to be here this evening; and, though I had the misfortune to belong to the minority party, as my friend Mr. Tarbox said, I never saw any discrimination on his part with reference to any member of the Senate during the three years which I had the honor of serving in that body. I always voted for Brother Gifford; and I presume I always should, if I was re-elected to that honorable position on any future occasion.

Mr. Gifford is very happy in the administration of his duties, from what he stated to you this evening of what qualities should characterize a public officer. Though he has belonged to the predominant party of the State, he has always been elected in part by the votes of the minority; for, if a part of the majority becomes disaffected with a clerk or any other officer, he is easily thrown out of office, if the minority are also dissatisfied. But he so discharged his duties that he always served the minority and served the majority also. I trust, as has been said here to-night, that he will serve as long as he desires to serve, and I have no doubt that he will. His make-up is such that he will serve as long as he is able to serve; and, from his appearance here to-night, which is about the same as when I entered the Senate, in 1868, I think he may serve twenty-five years longer. [Applause.]

THE PRESIDENT (who had resumed the chair).— Gentle-men, I am reminded the hour is getting somewhat late, especially for Senators. There are many we should desire to hear from, if we had time; but, by the advice of those having charge of the meeting, and with great reluctance, I now declare it closed.